# Greater Is He

Joyce A. Wilson

Sierra Leonean Writers Series

**Greater Is He**



ISBN: 979-88461-50-69-0

**Sierra Leonean Writers Series**
Freetown; Warima, Sierra Leone
Publisher: Prof. Osman Sankoh (Mallam O.)
www.sl-writers-series.org
publisher@sl-writers-series.org

Dedicated to my grandchildren:

Charlotte, Enzi, Anissa and Amaya.

I pray that God's greatness will be manifested in your lives.

## ACKNOWLEDGEMENTS

My thanks and praise go first and foremost to Almighty GOD for the divine enablement and inspiration to produce a work of this nature. I give him all the praise and glory while holding on to the hope that this work would serve the purpose of "drawing men unto him as he is lifted up."

Next, I thank my dear husband Gerald, not only for his encouragement but also for helping me type the manuscript.

I also thank my children: Odunayo, Kristy, Omar and Ngozi for helping to provide the logistics without which this work would not have become a reality.

Finally, I thank my sister Dr. Fenela Avokey for urging and encouraging me to write.

I register my sincere thanks to you all and pray for God's richest blessings on your lives.

# PROLOGUE

"GREATER IS HE THAT IS IN ME, THAN HE THAT IS IN THE WORLD"

The whole purpose of the Christian life is to be molded into the image of Jesus Christ. Just as nature exhibits different seasons, so also the person who surrenders his or her life to God goes through different seasons of life during which he or she is exposed to different conditions that serve to shape his or her character into what God, the potter, wants he or she to become.

In nature, the Christian is exposed to the elements like wind, sun, snow and rain. In the same way God takes believers through different seasons of life during which we experience calm or stormy weather. These act on one's character to refine one into the image of Christ, which is the ultimate aim. This is a lifelong process which never ends, but culminates in the afterlife.

This novel seeks to explore how with God in control of the believer's life through the Holy Spirit, he or she can navigate the course of life, sailing through the seasons, be it calm or stormy weather. What determines the success of this journey is the presence of God in the believer's life. Thus, the title GREATER IS HE. God through the Holy Spirit is greater than the enemy of our souls who is in the world.

The aim of this work is to encourage readers to surrender their lives to God so that the Holy Spirit can guide them victoriously through all the differing circumstances of life. It also aims to motivate new believers to grow in faith so they would observe God's power at work with the resultant effect of them completely surrendering their lives to God. For those who are already committed Christians it is hoped that this work will spur them on to a closer walk with God and see him manifest his power in greater ways in their lives.

Moreover, the institution of marriage seems to be under threat. Couples these days are not patient with each other and are more often than not, eager to opt for divorce. This novel therefore targets young married couples with a view towards encouraging them to put God at the center of their marriages as this would set them on the right footing and ensure the success of their marriages.

It also aimed at single people who hope to get married and seeks to prepare them for the pitfalls of married life. Finally, it is hoped that even those who prefer to remain single would benefit from this work as it should encourage them to live upright lives and so contribute to the restoration of a society gone haywire, that needs to rediscover its moral compass.

# CHAPTER 1

Ava Sommers is the beautiful, smart and confident only daughter of Winston and Marion Sommers. Her best friend, Vida Gaines, who lives next door, is fun loving, though more of an introvert, and the older child of Joseph and Yvette Gaines. A friendship that budded in second grade has endured over the years. Both girls are fifteen and are now becoming aware of the world around them, of relationships and of what society expects of them.

"Hey Vida! We have Inspire Night at our church next Friday. Would you care to attend? My mum and I can pick you up and drop you off after it ends."

"Let me ask my parents if they would let me attend. I would very much like to though."

Winston and Marion Sommers are both born again Christian believers who are striving to bring up their daughter according to the tenets of the Christian faith. Vida however is not so fortunate as her parents

Joseph and Yvette Gaines do not have a relationship with God. They believe that all they possess and have achieved are due mainly to their own efforts. Not surprisingly they are not enthusiastic when Vida seeks their permission to attend the Inspire Night. Vida had to inform a disappointed Ava that she could not attend.

Inspire Night turns out to be a momentous evening with many people coming to faith in Christ among whom was Ava Sommers.

"How did it go last Friday Ava? So sorry I could not make it," a sad Vida enquires when she sees Ava in school on Monday.

"Oh! it was wonderful, and the good news is that I actually gave my life to Christ." "You did?" an excited Vida responds." Wish I was there. I might have done the same."

"Don't worry Vida, there will be more opportunities. Perhaps your parents will allow you to attend in future."

The Gaines' marriage is experiencing some tumultuous times. After fifteen years of marriage during which there have been endless fights, the couple seems to be getting to the end of their tether. This unrest in the home seems to be having a negative effect on their children, Vida and her younger brother Simon. Vida, the more sensitive one is suffering emotionally and finds it hard to concentrate in school when she thinks about the toxic atmosphere at home. Her teacher, Mrs. Stone, points this out to Mrs. Gaines when she attends the Parent-Teacher conference at school. She explains that her grades are declining as a result of the instability in the home. She emphasized the point that to perform well children need a peaceful and stable atmosphere.

Yvette attempts to discuss this issue with her husband, but this leads to another fight as each try to blame the other Vida's poor performance. These fights continue and they increase in frequency and intensity. They would sometimes go for long periods without uttering a word to each other. This is really not an ideal situation as it takes its toll on the marriage and on their children, who begin to feel insecure, particularly as they do not receive encouragement and affirmation from their parents.

Things continue like this and Yvette suggests that they see a marriage counsellor to which Joseph does not acquiesce. He believes they should be able to sort out their differences themselves. This however does not seem feasible at this point and things continue to deteriorate in their relationship. It gets to the point where they begin to consider divorce. Joseph wants out while Yvette thinks their differences can be reconciled.

Finally, Joseph files for divorce, which after some proceedings, is granted on the grounds of incompatibility and irreconcilable differences. Custody of Vida is given to Yvette, the mother, while Simon the son goes to the father. Had they nourished a relationship with God, things would most likely not have taken this turn. Now that Yvette has the option of raising Vida up by herself, will things be different? Will Vida's grades improve? However, they should be fine economically as Joseph has to pay child support for

Vida. What about the fatherly influence in a child's life? This would be lacking, and it is often not easy to fill this emotional void.

Ava on the other hand continues to thrive. The stability in her home and the loving support of praying parents ensure good grades and overall excellent performance for her.

A heartbroken Vida confides in her friend Ava in school one day.

"I wish my parents were still together. I miss my dad very much and I can tell that my Mum is not happy. She is lonely. I try to comfort her, but I just don't know what to say."

Ava herself is at a loss for words as she just cannot think of suitable words to say. She puts a comforting hand around her friend and encourages her not to think too much about the situation.

## CHAPTER 2

Winston comes home on a Friday evening from work looking rather dejected and worn out.

"Why are you wearing such a long face, darling?" his wife Marion enquires.

"My dear, work is not going too well. As you know I think I am overdue for a promotion, but nothing is being said about it. When I tried to discuss the issue with my boss, he merely changed the subject."

"I perfectly understand how you feel, my dear. Don't be so downcast, however. Your time will come. Things always happen according to God's perfect timing for his children. Let's keep praying about it. God is never a minute early, nor a minute late. He will surely come through for you." Marion reassures him.

"Thanks for the encouragement my dear. I am working very hard, but I guess I just have to be patient and keep trusting God. What would I do without you my dear? By the way my dear, do you think you are up to entertaining next weekend? I was thinking of inviting a colleague of mine to dinner. He is new in town as he has just accepted a position at our company. I am sure he would like to come with his fiancée."

"No problem my dear. You know I am always game when it comes to entertaining. Moreover, I am always happy when God brings people into our lives that we can share his love with."

"That settles it. His name is Melvin, and his fiancée is Alberta.

"By the way, what's the latest regarding the purchase of our new home? Did you get any correspondence from the realtors?"

"Oh yeah, I got some mail about it yesterday, but you were so tired when you came home, I decided to shelve it until the weekend. Things are on course and we are expected to visit the showcase of houses on Sunday to help us make up our minds as to which one we want. The houses are in a new area that is being developed and I believe we will like it."

It is Friday evening and Melvin and Alberta arrive at the Sommers' for dinner. Introductions are made, and they settle down to a pleasant evening of chit chat. Alberta is thirty-one and has just emigrated from Sierra Leone, West Africa. She won a diversity lottery, and this has enabled her to move to the United States as her new home. She met Melvin soon after arrival and they struck up a relationship that is thriving.

As we can well imagine, the evening turns out to be very interesting. Alberta tells about her childhood and teenage years in Sierra Leone while eagerly listening to her American hosts talk about life in America, her new home. The differences in culture between America and her native Sierra Leone cannot be overemphasized. She tells with passion, stories of war and carnage that she witnessed during a senseless civil war that raged in her homeland in the 1990's.

"It all started on a Sunday afternoon, "Alberta began, "when it was reported that there had been an attack on a town in the hinterland of our small West African country. Apparently, a gang of bandits had crossed over from the Liberian border and attacked a village, pillaging, burning down homes and killing the villagers. This signaled the start of a war that would spread its tentacles to all the districts in the country and finally reach the capital city."

"How did you survive in such dire circumstances?" an astonished Marion quizzed.

"It was during that period that I came to know the Lord Jesus Christ and that was what saved and sustained me."

A familiar chord was struck in the conversation and the Sommers naturally wanted to hear how her faith had enabled her to weather the storms of carnage and adversity as a vulnerable young lady.

"I attended prayer meetings regularly during which prayers were offered for the country. It was during one such prayer meeting that I accepted Christ as my Lord and Savior and this relationship sustained me during those difficult years.

There was complete breakdown of law and order and twelve-year-old boys could be seen toting rifles they could hardly carry. Food was scarce as farmers were petrified of being massacred in their farms and their crops stolen. The capital city became densely populated as people from the provinces moved to areas considered safer. Consequently, amenities like electricity and potable water could not meet the increased demand and they began to crumble.

A country that had made little progress since independence was plunged into a state of anarchy from which she would take decades to recover. With the help of friendly countries however, order was restored, the renegade army was disbanded and life returned to near normal."

Meanwhile, Alberta grew in her relationship with Christ and she saw many miraculous answers to her prayers. Some people went without food for days during the height if the unrest. There was not a single day, however, that people in her family went without food. Their home was not burnt down, nor did they suffer any physical abuse. God is always faithful, and he took good care of them.

All too soon, the evening came to an end and Melvin and Alberta had to leave.

They thanked their hosts graciously and took their leave.

# CHAPTER 3

The relationship between Winston and Marion continues to blossom. However, they face trials in their jobs, and this is a source of concern for both of them. Winston's promotion for which he is due does not seem to be forthcoming. His boss simply avoids discussing the issue. Finances in the family are tight and the promotion would ensure more liquidity. Life is never a bed of roses. What do we do when we keep on lifting an issue to God and there seems to be no answer? Winston is a hard worker, a good team player and someone committed to the ideals of the company he works for. Why then was his promotion being stalled? This is the question he asks repeatedly to which no answers come. He and Marion decide to continue praying about it and waiting on God to act on their behalf. They purpose to be praying for his boss as well. They do not know what problems he may be experiencing, and they reckon that praying for him could only help the solution.

For her part, Marion works as a teacher in a private school. She would also like to have an increase in her wages to augment the family income. The school however for which she works does not seem to be attracting a lot of students. This, it is believed, is because of the competition with other private schools in the area. Consequently, the school does not realize much financially to justify a raise in the teachers' salaries. Thus, this also is a standing prayer request during their prayer time.

In their journey with God, they are also learning from the situation in their jobs that a relationship with God does not mean that they would be devoid of problems. Life is not a straight road. There are usually twists and turns. However, keeping our hands in the hands of the Savior helps us to navigate these twists and turns and come out victorious.

Ava, meanwhile, is growing in her faith and her relationship to Christ having accepted him as her Lord and Savior. She continues to excel in her schoolwork and is a source of pride and joy to her parents. She continues to take a keen interest in her friend who indeed is having a rough time growing in a broken home. She believes in Vida, and despite her situation, she will always be her best friend.

Vida's father, Joseph Gaines is a very good provider however and does not fail to pay the child support. So materially, Vida is not in want. Joseph also seems to be excelling in his job lending credence to the adage "what we lose in the swings we gain in the roundabout." He may have lost his marriage, but God cares about him too and he is making a headway in his job, even though he is not yet a Christian.

Yvette Gaines works as a nurse and her job is what keeps her going but her evenings are lonesome as she feels the need for company particularly when Vida is occupied with her homework. Should she get into another relationship if the opportunity presents itself? She also begins to ponder about her relationship to God. Should she turn to God? Would he fill the void in her life?

David Smith is also a nurse at the facility in which

Yvette works. They have a good relationship as colleagues, but he never crossed her mind as a potential partner. David is a Charismatic Christian, on fire for the Lord. He notices that Yvette seems forlorn and withdrawn in some ways and this has started having an impact on her job. She is not her normal caring self as she was accustomed to being, and even the old folks at the care facility for which she works begin to notice the change in her disposition. David decides to talk to Yvette about this and to witness to her, presenting Jesus Christ to her as one who can meet her emotional and spiritual needs.

"You are not your usual jovial self, Yvette. What's eating you up these days? Care to talk about it?"

"Well, David, you may not have heard about it, but I got divorced a couple of months ago."

"Oh, really? So sorry to hear that. Don't take it too hard though, you'll get over it. How's your spiritual life? Do you go to church? Are you saved?"

"Well," replies Yvette "I used to be a churchgoer but when I got married, I slacked off about it as my husband did not like going to church."

"But have you thought of starting again, now that he is out of your life?" David pressed.

"It has actually crossed my mind, but I have been putting it off." "Maybe I need to give it a try once more."

There is a Charismatic church not too far from where Yvette lives and she resolves to start going there the following Sunday. When she tells Vida about it, she is overjoyed. She thinks of her friend Ava who is a Christian and would like to be one herself.

Come Sunday, a very excited Vida gets ready even before her mum, so they could go to church. The service lasted for just an hour, but Yvette comes away from it feeling refreshed and happy that they had gone. There were worshippers there who welcomed them warmly and they felt very much at home. The preacher, the pastor of the church based his sermon on John 3:16 – "For God so loved the world that he gave his only son that whosoever believed in him should not perish but have eternal life".

He explained that we need to give our lives to Christ and become saved. This would qualify us for eternal life. Yvette was enthralled for the whole duration of the sermon. This was to her good news. God loves her and wants to be her friend. She decides to give it serious thought after which she would decide what to do.

"Guess what Ava" says an excited Vida on Monday. "My mum and I went to church yesterday. I guess I am on my way to becoming a Christian after all." "Oh Vida, I am so happy for you. You will never regret it"

Both Yvette and Vida continue to attend church services regularly and after about three months they both responded to an altar call and surrendered their lives to Jesus. They experienced a joy they had never felt before and Vida is anxious to report to her friend, Ava, in school on Monday.

"I know that feeling very well" says Ava when

her friend describes to her how she felt on receiving Christ as her personal savior. "You experience the joy that you now have, that comes from someone loving you unconditionally just the way you are."

## CHAPTER 4

Joseph Gaines, despite the fact that he is doing well in his job and making good headway with his career, begins to feel that there must be more to life than just going to work and hanging out with friends. He feels lonely and unfulfilled and there is no one in his circle of friends that he can confide in. They are all without exception single men who are averse to marriage as they believe it robs men of their freedom. They are content with dating multiple women and they consider marriage too restrictive. Joseph has experimented with marriage and has opted out. So naturally, even though he is unhappy, he does not see marriage as the answer.

Soon he begins to drift from the norm of dating women and starts dating men in the hope that this would bring him happiness. He keeps this a secret from his main group of friends as he seems to think they may not approve of it. Is he making a good choice? In life we always have to live with the consequences of our choices which is why we always have to ensure we make good choices. Moreover, diseases like HIV AIDS have been found to be prevalent among people engaging in alternate lifestyles. For now, Joseph feels he is on the right path. The Word of God says however:

"There is a way that seems right unto a man but the end thereof is destruction." In Romans 1:26-27, God's word condemns same gender sexual relations. Many people, some of whom may be churchgoers are not conversant with the scriptures and consequently flout God's commands. There is a need to become practicing Christians well-versed in his word and heeding his instructions for right living. It is amazing how many prominent people, opinion leaders and public figures are now living these alternate lifestyles. Sooner or later God's ire would be provoked and who knows whether he might not want to treat such people as he did the Biblical Sodom and Gomorrah.

One cannot help but wonder what values are being passed on to the next generation, that they in turn would pass on to their children and to posterity. Timeless values which should make for a wholesome society are being eroded and not much is being done to salvage them. Something needs to be done to forestall the disintegration of society. The traditional marriage system between a man and woman is under threat and something must be done to salvage it.

## CHAPTER 5

Winston plods on despite the stalling of his promotion at his place of work. Encouraged by his wife Marion, he endeavors to draw even nearer to God. He takes the initiative and starts a Men's Fellowship group at his church with the aim of getting members to grow to maturity in their relationship with God and to pursue right living.

The fellowship is open to all men in the church aged thirty and above. They hold bible study sessions during which they pore over the word of God in a bid to get the men conversant with it particularly as it pertains to their moral lives. They are encouraged to have a right relationship with God, be upright family men and exhibit integrity in their places of work.

Knowledgeable men of God are sometimes invited to give talks to them based on the word of God. On one occasion, a speaker was invited who gave a talk on the topic– Obedience to the Word of God. It turns out to be a very lively session that culminated in a question and answer period. Apart from dwelling on the Ten Commandments, the speaker makes reference to other parts of the Bible with which people are not so conversant. Proverbs 5, in which men are counselled about sexual relations attracts a lot of attention. Most of the men admit that they were not aware of this chapter.

"Drink water only from your own well. Share your love only with your wife."

Why spill the water of your springs having relations with just anyone. [NLT].

These issues are thoroughly discussed, and the men's eyes are opened to the dictates of God's word. This of course is contrary to popular culture of believing that it is macho to have mistresses or side-chicks. The speaker points out to them that the way of God is the way of wisdom. When one fears God there are certain things he will not indulge in.

"Love wisdom like a sister, make insight a beloved member of your family. Let them hold you back from an affair with an immoral woman, from listening to the flattery of an adulterous woman. "Proverbs 7:4-5[NLT]

On another occasion, they have a panel discussion on "The merits of Integrity." Thus, Winston is being used by God as an instrument to nurture these men, not only to be good husbands and fathers but also workers with integrity in their places of work and in society.

# CHAPTER 6

Marion is also a member of the Women's Ministry at their church. It is a vibrant ministry in which the women encourage each other to live meaningful Christian lives while ministering to the needs of their families and community. They hold regular monthly meetings at the church hall mostly but sometimes in the homes of members. Members are encouraged to develop their God-given potentials and mature into women of substance comparable to the woman of noble character described in Proverbs 31. Women who would meaningfully complement their husbands, raise godly children and be important contributors to a wholesome society.

"Who can find a virtuous and capable wife. She is worth more than precious rubies. Her husband can trust her, and she will greatly enrich his life. "( Proverbs 31: 10- 11.

"Her children stand and bless her. Her husband praises her." Proverbs 31:28

"Charm is deceptive, and beauty does not last but a woman who fears the Lord will be greatly praised. Let her deeds publicly declare her praise." Proverbs 31:30-31.

Apart from encouraging the women to live Godly lives, they are challenged to raise funds that are used to spread God's love among people in their community. For instance, every Christmas season, they would pull their resources together and fete the children in their community, feeding them physically while bringing God's word to them. Clothes would also be distributed to them.

At other times, orphanages or disabled people would be fed as well provided clothes. These women also make their own contributions to the furnishing of the new church edifice that is being built.

The older women are encouraged to mentor the younger women as the word of God instructs. Sisterly love is fostered, and this ministry goes a long way in providing a support system for the women as they go through the different seasons of life - joy or sorrow, rain or shine.

Through daily devotions posted on the Ministry's forum, the women are helped to become mature Christians- becoming women of faith who approach life and all it brings, with the calm resolve that they serve a God who is in control of the universe and who is able to meet one's needs when one has a meaningful relationship with him.

Due to this atmosphere of Christian love that the women share, there is noticeably no petty quarrels or squabbles often present in women's circles.

This ministry even impacts the marriages and family life of these women. They mature as Christian ladies, who are submissive to their husbands as the word dictates. They do not retaliate in cases where their husbands are guilty of infidelity but rather go on their knees for them and with time, their spouses tend to come to their senses and the marriage is restored.

## CHAPTER 7

Simon, Vida's brother seems to be having a rough deal. He misses his Mom terribly and begins to look for love and acceptance in the wrong places.

"Hey Simon!" a friend hails him after school one day. "Come with me, I want you to meet some friends of mine."

Feeling bored, and not wanting to be left out, he accompanies his friend instead of going home after school. This friend introduces him to a group of his own friends. Simon, being extremely naïve and unsuspecting is not aware that he was being introduced to a gang. He joins them and was soon initiated into smoking marijuana. He could not resist as he felt the need to belong. Smoking the drug soon becomes a habit and he begins to crave more and more of it to the point that even the pocket money given to him by his Dad could not support the habit.

He turns to his newfound friends for a solution. Having been in this for a while, they quickly show him the ropes. They, for some time had been involved in shoplifting and Simon is now initiated into this deviant act. They rob shops and supermarkets, sell their items to older drug addicts at next to nothing prices and that way he is able to support his new lifestyle.

Had he not been a product of a broken home, he more likely than not would have had his parent's unconditional love and would not have had to seek acceptance or a sense of belonging from a gang. He was however in deep waters right now and according to the age old adage, he had to swim or sink. He often thinks about his sister Vida and wonder how she is faring.

There is something to be said for parents once they are in the marriage relationship. They need to be more patient with each other more so for the sake of the children who are usually the worst affected when they go apart. Things get out of hand very quickly when Simon continues to associate with this gang. On a particular occasion they decide to shoplift in a supermarket and Simon and one other boy were caught by the security guards in the store and handed over to the police.

One cannot begin to imagine Joseph's shock when he got a call summoning him to the Police Station and he arrived and met his son Simon under arrest. When Simon was interrogated, his new lifestyle and gang membership became known to his father as the Police briefed him regarding what he had been up to. Being a first-time offender, he is cautioned and released with the understanding that he needed to mend his ways. The force of the gang on him however is so strong that he finds it extremely difficult to extricate himself from them. With some of these things, only the power of fervent prayer can serve to accomplish this severance.

## CHAPTER 8

Settling down in the USA is no child's play. Alberta however receives much needed help from friends like the Sommers and Melvin who gave her helpful tips regarding choosing an apartment, finding a job and so on. Her relationship with Melvin seems smooth sailing and they get on well together.

Finding a job however proves to be a huge challenge for her. Back in her native land she used to work as a sales clerk for a mobile phone company. She did not possess any significant professional qualifications to stand her in good stead in the job market in the States. She now considers furthering her education and settling down in a profession. She decides to go into the medical field and train as a nurse. This involves a lot of study hours and she sets herself the goal to qualify in a couple of years.

In order to raise money to pay for her program, she took a job at a Dunkin Donuts restaurant, a stone's throw from where she stayed. She put in long hours and was able to save quite a good deal although she would still have to be working while pursuing her studies. This she considers a lucky break as it is possible for her to work and study at the same time

Classes for her started online and since there is virtually no social life, she spends a lot of time studying and keeping up with homework. She sees Melvin only on weekends and as such her grades are very good as she puts in a lot of effort into her work. In recognition of her hard work, she is offered a part scholarship which covers seventy percent of her tuition fees. This is most welcome for her as it is something she had been praying about. She ensures that now that she is on her own, she does not stray from the Christian faith to which she had become committed. She attends church regularly. She also watches televangelists like Joyce Meyer, Joel Austin etc. and these activities serve to bolster her faith. She chooses her friends wisely being extremely cautious not to choose friends who would cause her to stray from the faith. She is aware that peer pressure can affect not only children but adults as well. As the Bible says

"Can two work together unless they be agreed"

Her relationship with Christ is of immense importance to her and she does all in her power to preserve this link.

## CHAPTER 9

The Sommers invite Alberta to their church where she feels very much at home. She soon joins the Women's Ministry which becomes a veritable support group for her. One admirable practice of the Women's Ministry is that of reaching out to needy people in the community. They operate a soup kitchen for the less fortunate as well as a clothes closet. Alberta and Marion, now fast friends always volunteer to serve in these outreach activities. The women of the ministry all participate eagerly and always testify about the fulfillment they have in being channels for God's grace to people who are sometimes in dire need or desperate circumstances.

Alberta also volunteers to be a Sunday School Teacher. There being an over subscription of volunteers, she gets to serve in this capacity twice a month. These outlets- The Men's Fellowship, The Women's Ministry and The Sunday School all serve to weld the church community together into a warm fellowship of believers. Through these arms church members not only enrich their relationship with God, brotherly love, nurturing and caring is also fostered among them. Sunday attendance at services is certainly not enough. These arms help to create a sense of belonging to a church family.

Ava Sommers, being talented and a very hard worker excels in school. She shines as the star of the day in her school's prize giving ceremony when she wins proficiency prices as well as special prizes. Her proud parents are in attendance and are pleasantly surprised at the sheer number of prizes she wins. Among her prizes is one for reliability. Her ability to maintain decorum in her class as a class prefect, particularly in the absence of the teacher earns her this prize. At such an early age she exhibits admirable leadership skills. All this coupled with her academic prowess can be attributed to the stable, cordial and enabling home environment in which she is being raised.

Ava belongs to the Sunday school in her church and is actively growing in the things of God.

Moreover, she is being brought up in the tradition where daily family prayers are a must.

Winston and Marion continue to lift their concerns regarding their respective professions to the Lord. After many years of waiting in faith, God comes through for them and Winston receives the long-anticipated promotion which had been stalled. This brings with it added income to the family coffers which would enable them to afford certain necessities they had hitherto gone without. They are also able to lay some funds aside in preparation for Ava's tertiary education. Indeed, their case demonstrates that God always comes through for his children. All that is needed is faith, trust and patience as one awaits the appointed time.

# CHAPTER 10

Yvette now gets to the point where she realizes that something ought to be done about Joseph who was reneging on his child support payments. For a period of six months nothing was paid, and she had to rely only on her own income for the sustenance of herself and their daughter Vida.

She also has some anxiety about their son Simon when she learns that he is into drugs and gangs. Since she is now a Christian, she decides to bring these concerns to God in prayer on a daily basis. She does not want to resort to legal action against Joseph as she believes that neither Joseph nor Simon is beyond redemption and legal action would create additional strain in what are already very difficult family dynamics. After all God's word says:

"It is not his will that any should perish, but that all should come to a saving knowledge of his grace."

In life however, things often seem to get

worse before it gets better. So, she continues interceding for them. She also finds it in her heart to forgive him for the hurtful utterances he had made during the divorce proceedings. She also believes that Joseph's turnaround when it does happen will have a positive impact on Simon.

During her weekly conversations with Simon, she tries to counsel him in the hope that he will drop his drug and gang habits.

After some time, God answers her prayers, and she gets a call from Joseph who asks her to forgive his lapses in paying the child support. He explains that he had been going through a rough patch, but things are looking up now. He resumes payment of the child support and Yvette rejoices about the way her prayers have been answered. This serves to increase her faith in God and reassure her that God is indeed a prayer-answering God.

This also encourages her to continue in prayers for Simon believing that he would mend his ways soon and may even come to a saving knowledge of Christ, for "With God all things are possible to him who believes."

## CHAPTER 11

Alberta continues with her nursing course and actually excels in it. With the help of funds gleaned from the job at Dunkin Doughnuts and the scholarship, she sees herself through and graduates with honors after four years.

Melvin saves as much as he can as he plans to settle down in marriage to Alberta. He chooses the very day of Alberta's graduation to propose to her. So, it was a day of double joy for Alberta. She gladly accepts his offer of marriage and after a few months of planning and preparation they get married in a civil ceremony in court followed by a reception at the civic center in their town.

Among the honored guests in attendance were Winston and Marion Sommers and their daughter Ava as well as other well-wishers from Alberta's church where she dutifully serves as a Sunday school teacher. Having had a courtship or dating period of four years, Alberta is convinced that marriage to Melvin is a step in the right direction.

The only wild card that she could see is that Melvin is not yet a committed Christian. He goes to church occasionally, but he has not yet committed his life to Christ. She had started praying for him and has the firm belief that someday soon, he would become born again and together they can build a Christian home. She admires the Sommers who have a very successful marriage largely due to the fact that they have Jesus Christ at the center of their home. There are so many people out there who can so readily be used by the evil one to seduce one's spouse and cause them to go contrary to their marital vows. Alberta has friends back home in her native land whose marriages have not thrived just because of third party interference. She therefore decides to be praying regularly that this should not be her lot. She reckons that if Melvin becomes a committed Christian, it would be easier for the two to be praying together for their marriage. She longs for the time when it will be so.

Meanwhile she gets a job at the hospital nearby

where they stay, and she immerses herself in her job and homemaking.

## CHAPTER 12

Ava and Vida continue as friends. They have mutual interests to chat about now that they are both Christians. Moreover, they are also able to discuss their schoolwork. Despite the fact that Vida misses her Dad, she is doing a lot better now in her academic work. This can be attributed to the fact that there are no more fights to sadden or distract her. She has her mother's love and full attention and so she seems to be thriving now.

Christian Youth Leaders play a pivotal role in the lives of these children. They are instrumental in organizing programs such as seminars, Inter Schools Quiz Competitions, Debates etc. These are all aimed at helping these children to become well rounded in their intellectual and spiritual development.

Student Christian Movements and Scripture Union Organizations are set up in schools and through these media, the good news of the Gospel is spread among the young people.

On one particular year Ava and Vida find

themselves on two opposing teams in a quiz competition. They had both been chosen to represent their respective schools. It was a Bible Quiz, and the teams were comprised of four contestants each. These participants were required to have a very good knowledge of the stories in the Bible thereby being very confident representatives of their schools. Questions are based on a knowledge of the life of Jesus, his parables and miracles, The Ten Commandments and other elements rudimentary to the Christian Faith.

As the contestants answer the questions, they are cheered on by an audience drawn from another school. The two teams are well-matched and the competition ends in a draw. They now have to face other teams from other schools and consequently the competition will culminate in the emergence of the champion who would be awarded the winner's shield. Ava's school had never won it before while Vida's had won it once. It is thus that these young people are nurtured spiritually. It is necessary to catch them young before the enemy of our souls does.

## CHAPTER 13

Sometimes in life, people get into situations where they become morally bankrupt before getting to the point where they come to realize that they need God in their lives.

For all intents and purposes, this is what happens to Joseph. Whenever he spoke to his ex, Yvette, he noted a peace and calm in her voice which he begins to covet. He meanwhile is miserable as he increasingly realizes that the freedom he had won with the divorce had not really made him happy. There was a void in his life which he tried to fill albeit unsuccessfully. He gets so miserable that he goes into a state of depression. It gets so bad that he had to see a therapist recommended by one of his colleagues whom he confides in.

He is able to unburden to the therapist and the sessions prove to be therapeutic for him. He begins to realize his need for God and to feel that only God can fill the void that exists in his heart. It is a proven fact that as human beings we possess a void that must be filled by a spiritual force since we are made of body, soul and spirit. A vacuum cannot exist in nature. It must be filled, and it is only when that void is filled by God that true happiness and fulfillment can be achieved in life.

Thus, Joseph thinks seriously about his relationship to God and he decides to start going to church. Lately he had become aware of Simon's deviant behavior also and this had got him very concerned that he could have been a terrible role model for the young boy. He therefore resolves that he would do all in his power to amend his ways in the hope that Simon will quit associating with gangs and drugs and would make a turnaround in his life.

Neither of them is aware that Yvette was consistently offering prayers for them. Joseph succeeds in convincing Simon to attend church with him. Soon they became members of a nearby Charismatic church and Joseph after a few months of attending together with Simon gave his life to Christ and is baptized. Joseph becomes a member of the Men's Fellowship and Simon attends Sunday School where he meets with his peers and forms friendships that help him to have a sense of belonging not to gangs this time but to brothers and sisters in the kingdom of God.

One cannot imagine Yvette's joy and happiness when she learns about the conversion of her former husband and son. Her faith and trust in God is rewarded as she sees answers to her prayers. She witnesses firsthand the great miracle of salvation in her husband and son's lives. Indeed "with God all things are possible" and it is not his will that any should perish but that all should come to a saving knowledge of his grace.

## CHAPTER 14

Melvin and Alberta have been married for four years now and they begin to become concerned that they have not yet reproduced an offspring. As some husbands sometimes do, Melvin begins to be attracted to other women. He feels he is lacking in that he has not yet fathered a child. Soon he is entrapped by a woman he meets through his job. As The Bible states "No man can serve two masters". Consequently, the relationship between him and Alberta begins to deteriorate.

By a stroke of chance, Alberta gets to know about this extramarital affair, and they have endless arguments when she confronts him about it. Alberta confides in a mature Christian married woman who advises her to refrain from confrontations that lead to arguments. She is also advised to be on the alert so that she is not tempted to retaliate and so fall into the same sin of adultery.

Melvin is not yet a born again Christian and like most men he sees nothing wrong in being unfaithful to his wife. Such men believe that men are considered macho when they have side chicks. For now, Melvin belongs to this category.

Alberta takes to heart the advice she gets from her older friend and desists from bringing up the issue to Melvin. Instead, she begins to pray fervently for Melvin. She herself continues to grow in her knowledge of God through attendance at Bible Studies and prayer meetings. She endeavors to be as good a wife as she can possibly be. She clings to the scripture in 1Peter 3:1 which states that by her good conduct even without a word, her husband can be won over.

Melvin, after a while begins to wonder about the change in Alberta. She no longer confronts him about his infidelity but ensures that he enjoys nourishing meals, a clean home as well as her companionship. He admires the calmness, poise and composure that Alberta exudes. He does not experience the happiness he had hoped for in engaging in an illicit affair.

At the same time, he also begins to realize that

he was spending money unnecessarily on the illicit relationship as this other woman expects him to pay her bills and lavish expensive gifts on her. He should be thinking of putting funds aside towards the purchase of their own home.

# CHAPTER 15

Winston and Marion continue to thrive in their jobs. Ava and Vida are now in different schools having proceeded to High School. They are still very good friends as they meet in church and in Inter Schools activities.

These girls now aged fifteen enter a season of their lives when they are now adolescents. They begin to assert themselves and to take an interest in the opposite sex. Parents at this stage often wonder how to handle their children during this delicate season of their lives.

Being an only child Winston and Marion are particularly worried about Ava. Naturally, they want her to turn out just right. This concern is accentuated when she becomes a victim of bullying. Some of her classmates notice how seriously she takes her relationship with God and they begin to call her names such as "Holy Mary" to make her uncomfortable. She confides in her mother who takes it up with her teacher.

The culprits are given stern warnings and they henceforth desist. They however shun her and would not have much to do with her. She hears of some of the girls in her class having relationships with the opposite sex and she begins to feel that she is missing out. She feels ill at ease, thinking that she is not welcome among her peers. She feels the strong pull of peer pressure. This is a crucial stage in her development. Her mother realizing this, counsels her consistently, helping her to realize and accept that it is fine if one does not follow the crowd.

She explains to Ava that even adults sometimes have a hard time resisting peer pressure. There is always this desire to feel a sense of belonging and to feel accepted. Ava also discovers that her friend Vida is facing similar struggles in her school. Vida's mother Yvette counsels her daughter along the same lines as Marion and moreover enlists the assistance of the social worker at Vida's school.

It does help when these two friends come to realize that they have each other and their mothers for support. They are made to realize that in this season of their lives, their main concern should be their education. Relationships with the opposite gender would always come later. As the writer of Ecclesiastes states:
"There is a time for every purpose under heaven,"

Fortunately, these hiccups do not affect the girls' performance and they continue to perform well in their respective schools.

## CHAPTER 16

Simon meanwhile had recovered from the downward spiral occasioned by indulgence in drugs and being a member of a gang. He however misses his mother so much that he prevails on his father to allow him to take advantage of the visiting rights that had been accorded to him during the divorce settlement.

His mother arranges an outing together with his sister Vida and the three of them go on an outing to a nearby beach resort. Yvette seizes this singular opportunity to talk to and counsel Simon. Simon had really not found happiness as a member of a gang and his mother explained to him that true happiness can only be found in a relationship with Jesus. He listens attentively as his mother explained to him how she herself had accepted Christ and the difference that was making in her life.

Simon agrees to give it serious thought and would communicate his decision on his next visit. Meanwhile he confesses to his mother that his greatest wish is for his parents to reconcile and get back together. He also informs his mother that both he and his father have started going to church and that he is now a member of the Sunday school. Soon after this visit, he decides to quit the gang much to the chagrin of his gang mates. He is resolute however and one cannot imagine the joy of Yvette on his next visit when he announces that he had quit the gang. Yvette continues praying convinced that it is only a matter of time before Simon turns over his life to Christ. Indeed, when Christians operate in the righteousness of God, their prayers are answered according to the word of God.

"The effective prayer of a righteous man avails much."

This change in Simon has a welcome impact on his overall comportment as well as in his performance in his schoolwork. Simon was indeed rescued in time. This is exactly how some young people start going downhill and by the time they know what is happening, they find themselves in prison and their lives are tainted.

## CHAPTER 17

Melvin continues in his illicit affair, but Alberta does not give up on him and continues interceding for him. He himself is beginning to feel discontented with his life generally. His job begins to betray his lack of concentration and devotion to it and his boss complains that he needs to be much more attentive in his work.

He confides in Alberta who encourages him to start praying about his concerns regarding his job. Oftentimes it happens that if we are just nominal Christians who transgress God's commands and do not live lives that please him, he according to his word will not prosper the work of our hands. Alberta discerns that this is what is happening in Melvin's life which is why she encourages him to seek the face of God.

A chord was struck, and Melvin heeds this advice. He loves his job and looks forward to making good headway in his career. He is a churchgoer but does not really have a relationship to God. God however being a merciful God answers his prayer and soon the situation in his job begins to improve. He also starts to consider having a relationship with Christ having begun to see answers to his prayers. God indeed must care for him and having a right relationship with him must be a step in the right direction.

"FOR GOD SO LOVED THE WORLD THAT HE GAVE HIS ONLY BEGOTTEN SON THAT WHOSOEVER BELIEVES IN HIM SHOULD NOT PERISH BUT HAVE EVERLASTING LIFE." John 3:16

What a promise! He gives a lot of thought to this and decides to do something about it. After hearing a sermon based on "The Prodigal Son" in Church on a particular Sunday, he was convicted and on his return home, he knelt down in the quiet of their bedroom and surrendered his life to Christ. He resolves to terminate his illicit affair, ask for God's pardon and forgiveness. He also asks for Alberta's forgiveness and determines to henceforth be faithful to God and to his wife.

Alberta, meanwhile, continues to be the best wife she could ever be. She refrains from alluding to his past infidelity as she is wise enough to know that this would serve no useful purpose other than generate strife in the home. She tries to be like the woman of noble character modelled in Proverbs 31.

As one can imagine, she is overjoyed to see the change that has come over Melvin and soon they begin to pray together lifting their concerns to God. The enemy of our souls is aware of the power at work when a committed Christian couple prays together. It is for this reason that he creates so many problems for marriages.

Melvin and Alberta are now determined not to allow him a foothold in their marriage and their relationship really blossoms as they find joy in each other's company like never before.

As one can imagine, foremost in their prayer points is that for an offspring. Soon this prayer is answered, and Alberta conceives and gives birth to a bouncing baby boy whom they name Melvin after his father. Their joy knows no bounds. This increases their faith in God. Indeed, God is great and is always faithful to those who put their trust in him.

## CHAPTER 18

With more income coming into their family coffers, Winston and Marion now decide to purchase the new home they had been dreaming about. They had been looking around and had located one in a nice suburb, not too far from their current residence.

It is a four bedroom, three and half bath home with a two-car garage. The asking price is within their reach and they are so excited that at least they would stop renting and move to their own home. Most excited in the family is Ava for whom this new home holds a bigger and more beautiful bedroom. She looks forward to her friend Vida coming over for sleepovers. Oh what fun they would have! There is also a spacious backyard where they can play games and have a lot of exercise.

Moving houses is not always an easy exercise. However, it is good to belong to a family of believers as when it is time for the Sommers to move to their new home, some friends from church came around to help them pack and move. Within a short time, they were able to move their items using a moving truck to the new home. They rested for the day and began to unpack the next day and began putting things in their proper places.

After a few days, they were feeling settled in their new home. They decide after a week to have a housewarming party to which they invite friends from work, church and their new neighbors. Their new house turns out to be a very lovely area with a park and lake within walking distance. A Mall with a wide diversity of shops and entertainment centers are also in the vicinity. They also find out that there is a nearby library with reading rooms in which one can spend leisure time and enjoy hours of quality time in the worlds encapsulated in books.

## CHAPTER 19

Not too long after moving, Marion begins to feel unwell and terribly under the weather. She attributes this to the stress of moving to their new house. She tries to rest but the feelings of fatigue become worse. She therefore decides to go for her annual checkup which was almost due. This indeed proves to be very timely as a mammogram reveals a lump in her left mammary gland.

She and her husband Winston take this news very calmly. They have seen God work wonders in their lives and are assured that this is just one more opportunity for him to glorify himself. According to God's word,

"Many are the afflictions of the righteous but the Lord delivers him out of them all."

They launch into fervent prayers and request prayer support from church members and friends who lovingly oblige.

The tumor which ended up being malignant becomes larger and Marion becomes really ill. They were told that surgery was the best option, and they begin to prepare themselves mentally for the procedure. Marion relies heavily on Biblical truths and quotes which bolster her faith and keep her in good spirits. She has never undergone surgery before and the tendency in such cases is to give in to fear.

Bouyed and encouraged by Winston and their strong faith in God, one of the quotes that she holds on to is the following:

"Do not be anxious about anything, but in every situation, by prayer and petition with thanksgiving, present your requests to God. And the peace of God which transcends all understanding, will guard your heart and minds in Christ Jesus." Phil 4:6-7.

The date is scheduled for the procedure and Marion goes to the Oncology Center where it would be done. Having fasted and prayed for a successful operation, Winston and Marion were convinced that all will go well. She was prepared and the procedure started.

However, halfway through the procedure there was a storm in the area which caused a power outage, something they had never experienced before in that facility. Evidently, the enemy of our souls was at work trying to cause problems. Due to ongoing prayer support, however, power was restored and the procedure was successfully completed. She comes around from the anesthesia to behold a beaming Winston by her bedside. They join hands and offer a prayer of thanksgiving to Almighty God for saving her life.

"INDEED, GREATER IS HE THAT IS IN US THAN HE THAT IS IN THE WORLD" 1 John 4:4

## EPILOGUE

Indeed, greater is he that is in us than he that is in the world. With God through the Holy Spirit indwelling the believer, he enjoys divine guidance, protection and provision. Believers can always count on God to meet them at their points of need. These needs may be spiritual, emotional, marital, health or otherwise. We need not navigate this life entirely on our own embattled by the enemy. Having a covenant relationship with Jesus ensures that we enjoy benefits such as protection, provision and healing.

Challenges will definitely arise as we are a fallen humanity but with God indwelling us, we are assured of his grace to see us through whatever comes our way.

To you who have read through this work, if you have not yet surrendered your life to Jesus Christ, you are hereby urged to do so. A close walk with him would definitely make a huge difference in this journey of life.

For you who are already in a relationship, continue to grow in your knowledge of him and experience that power that is greater than the one that is in the world. This would see you successfully through the seasons of life.

www.ingramcontent.com/pod-product-compliance
Lightning Source LLC
LaVergne TN
LVHW090126160826
845673LV00015B/1032